Text copyright © 1985 by Katharine Holabird
Illustrations copyright © 1985 by Helen Craig
All rights reserved.
Published in the United States in 1985 by Clarkson N. Potter, Inc.,
225 Park Avenue South, New York, New York 10003
and represented in Canada by the Canadian MANDA group.
First published in Great Britain by Aurum Press Ltd.
Clarkson N. Potter, Potter, and colophon
are trademarks of Clarkson N. Potter, Inc.
Manufactured in Singapore

Library of Congress Cataloguing in Publication Data
Holabird, Katharine
Angelina's Christmas.
Summary: Angelina and Cousin Henry bring
Christmas to a lonely old postman.
(1. Christmas-Fiction)   I. Craig, Helen ill.   II. Title.
PZ7.H689Ar 1985 (Fic) 85-12389
ISBN 0-517-57188-9

10 9 8 7 6 5 4 3 2 1

Angelina's Christmas

Illustrations by Helen Craig   Story by Katharine Holabird

Clarkson N. Potter, Inc./Publishers

Christmas was coming, and everyone at Angelina's school worked hard to prepare for the Christmas show. Angelina and the other children stayed after their lessons to rehearse and help decorate the hall.

When Angelina left school it was already dark outside. Large snowflakes were falling and Angelina was so excited that she danced along the pavement.

The cottages in the village looked warm and welcoming, with holly wreaths on the doors and Christmas lights shining in all the windows. But the very last cottage was cold and dark. Angelina peeped in the window and saw an old man huddled by a tiny fire.

Angelina ran the rest of the way home and found her
mother and little cousin Henry in the kitchen. She
asked her mother about the man who lived all alone
in the cottage.

"Oh, that's Mr Bell," her mother replied. "He used
to be the village postman, but he's too old to work now."

Angelina wanted to make a Christmas surprise for
Mr Bell, so Mrs Mouseling gave her some dough to make
cookies shaped like stars, bells and trees.

Henry had a piece of dough too, and he made a nice big Santa Claus cookie. "Look!" he said proudly. "I'm going to see Santa tonight and give him this cookie myself!"

"Santa only comes very late at night after everyone has gone to bed," Angelina explained. "Why don't you leave your cookie out on a plate for him?"

Henry started to cry. "No!" he shouted. "I want to see Santa Claus!"

"Don't be such a crybaby, Henry," Angelina scolded, but Henry didn't stop crying.

The next afternoon Angelina and her mother packed
a basket with the cookies and some mince pies and
fruit for Mr Bell. "Don't you want to help Angelina
take the presents to Mr Bell?" asked Mrs Mouseling,
but Henry only shook his head.

Then Angelina and her father went out to find a
Christmas tree for Mr Bell. Henry followed Angelina
and Mr Mouseling all the way to Mr Bell's cottage.
He still wouldn't say a word.

The old postman was amazed and delighted to see his visitors. He invited Angelina and her father inside. Then he noticed Henry standing alone in the snow. "Come in, my friend!" said Mr Bell with a smile.

Mr Bell's eyes were bright and twinkling. "Wait a moment," he said, and disappeared up the stairs.

Then he came down looking …

…just like SANTA CLAUS!

"This is the red costume I wore once when Santa Claus needed someone to take his place at the village Christmas party," said Mr Bell with a chuckle and he sat down and took Henry on his knee. While Mr Mouseling made tea and Angelina decorated the tree, Henry listened to Mr Bell's stories.

"I used to go out on my bicycle, no matter what the weather, to deliver presents to all the children in the countryside. One year there was a terrible blizzard. I had to deliver the toys on a sled, and if I hadn't glimpsed the village lights blinking in the distance I would have been lost in the storm."

Henry listened with wide eyes.

When it was time to go Henry reached into his pocket. "I made this," he said. "It's for you." Out of his pocket he took his big Santa Claus cookie and gave it to Mr Bell.

"This is the best Christmas surprise I've had for many years," said Mr Bell, thanking Henry and Angelina for their presents. Angelina said she wished Mr Bell would come to her school show in his Santa Claus costume.

"That would be a pleasure," he said, smiling.

So Mr Bell came in his red costume and watched the

sugar plum fairies dancing the Nutcracker Suite.

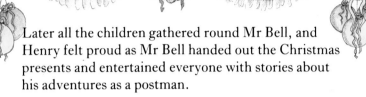

Later all the children gathered round Mr Bell, and
Henry felt proud as Mr Bell handed out the Christmas
presents and entertained everyone with stories about
his adventures as a postman.

Mr Bell was never lonely at Christmas again, because every year he was invited to come to Angelina's school in his Santa Claus suit for the Christmas show.